AKPA's
JOURNEY

Little ones—the world is full of questions, but if you listen closely, you will find that it is also full of answers.

For little S., who loves birds the best.

Published by Inhabit Media Inc.
www.inhabitmedia.com
Inhabit Media Inc. (Iqaluit) P.O. Box 11125, Iqaluit, Nunavut, X0A 1H0

Design and layout copyright © 2022 Inhabit Media Inc.
Text copyright © 2022 Mia Pelletier
Illustrations by Kagan McLeod copyright © 2022 Inhabit Media Inc.

Editors: Neil Christopher and Kelly Ward
Art Director: Danny Christopher

ISBN: 978-1-77227-429-5

Map on page 33 ©shutterstock.com/kateukraine

This project was made possible in part by the Government of Canada.

We acknowledge the support of the Canada Council for the Arts for our publishing program.

Library and Archives Canada Cataloguing in Publication

Title: Akpa's journey / by Mia Pelletier ; illustrated by Kagan McLeod.
Names: Pelletier, Mia, author. | McLeod, Kagan, illustrator.
Identifiers: Canadiana 20220237808 | ISBN 9781772274295 (hardcover)
Subjects: LCSH: Murres—Juvenile literature. | LCSH: Murres—Migration—Juvenile literature.
Classification: LCC QL696.C42 P45 2022 | DDC j598.3/3—dc23

Printed in Canada

AKPA'S JOURNEY

by Mia Pelletier

illustrated by Kagan McLeod

INHABIT MEDIA

In the beginning, there was an egg. The Arctic sun glowed through its speckled turquoise shell. A tiny murre named Akpa crouched inside, covered in wet feathers, almost ready to hatch.

Inside the egg, the world was small, and warm, and *quiet*. Akpa didn't know that his egg was one of many thousands of eggs balanced on the ledges of a high sea cliff. Or that each egg rested beneath the belly of a parent murre who sheltered it from wind and rain and guarded it from hungry egg thieves.

Egg thieves came to the sea cliffs one by one. First, an Arctic fox, lean from winter, picked his way down on nimble feet. As he climbed, he gobbled eggs up whole, but his stone stairs ran out before he reached the spot where Akpa grew.

Next came a hungry seagull, wheeling and crying on the wind. Its wings swept dark shadows across Akpa's shell, but his mother pushed the egg beneath her, hiding it from sight.

Last came a great white polar bear, climbing high along the cliffs. Up, up, *up* he climbed, up to the ledge where Akpa's egg lay. But the rock grew too steep and he could climb no further. His shaggy paw swept hungrily through empty air. Akpa's egg was just out of reach.

5

Akpa's parents took turns keeping their egg safe, and warm, and secret. And as the sun climbed higher in the sky each day, *manniit*, the springtime, passed. Still they waited for their egg to hatch.

One day, Akpa grew too large for his little egg. He knew it was time to peck a hole through the shell and peer outside. With one hard peck, a tiny crack appeared, and a warm sliver of golden light shone through. With a second peck the crack grew wider, and the shell fell open suddenly like a book.

Aarr-ahh! Aarr-ahh! The roar of the murre colony filled the air.

Pushing the shell aside, Akpa tottered up on skinny legs and stretched his downy wings to dry them. Far below, the icy ocean crashed and heaved. Akpa took one frightened look and drew in tight against his mother. *Akpa*, she cautioned as she tucked him safe beneath her wing, *stay close to me. Wait until you grow this big,* she said, brushing her bill across her belly, *then you will be ready to face the sea.*

Just as Akpa's feathers began to dry, his father flew in with a shining silver fish in his bill. Opening wide, Akpa swallowed the fish whole, filling his mouth with his first delicious taste of the sea. Now it was his mother's turn to fish, and his father's turn to keep him warm. *I'll be back soon*, she promised, as she flew out over the bright blue waves. Akpa watched the world from beneath his father's wing. High on the cliff tops, poppies swayed like sleepy dancers and fat bumblebees bobbed along on the salty breeze.

Before long, Akpa's mother returned with another tasty fish, and his father flew out, returning with yet another. The days passed like this, in an endless stream of gleaming fish.

Akpa grew and grew and *grew*.

One day, Akpa reached the place on his mother's belly that meant he was ready to face the sea. It was late summer, and the warmth of the sun was fading from the land. From farther north, the cold white winter would soon be reaching south, slowly stitching the waves together with ice.

It's time to go, Akpa's father said, looking out over the tossing sea. *We must keep ahead of the coming cold.*

But Papa, my feathers are only halfway grown! Akpa cried, holding out his stubby wings. *I can't fly yet!*

Akpa's father looked at his son with kind eyes. *This is the way for murres, his father explained. We are born near the sky, but first we must fall before we can fly. Your flying feathers will come, and the feathers you have now will keep you warm and dry. Your mother will fly south, and I will swim with you. As your feathers grow, I will trade my worn summer feathers for fresh winter ones and, for a while, neither of us will be able to fly. We'll swim together. I will teach you how to fish and show you the way to our winter home.*

But Papa! Akpa cried. *How will I reach the sea?*

Sometimes you have to leap when you can't yet fly, his father said, *and trust that the wind will carry you. We'll wait until dark,* he reassured his son, *when the seagulls are sleeping.*

As night fell, Akpa inched closer and closer to the cliff edge, peering down at the black waves crashing far below. In the dark, all distances are swallowed up, and it didn't seem so far from here to there. As the moon rose, its light glinted silver on the waves, and the air all around began to hum with the sound of leaping chicks. Akpa watched as, one by one, father murres jumped with their chicks, keeping pace in the air so they would land together on the sea.

Are you ready? Akpa's father asked. Akpa took a deep, brave breath. Then, before he could lose his courage, he squeezed his eyes shut tight, ran to the cliff ledge, and leapt! As his feet left the ledge, his father leapt too.

Akpa fell though the inky dark, down and down and *down* until. . . .

Splash! Akpa landed in a churning sea of chicks, each crying out for its father.

Papa! Akpa cried, feeling lost in the wet blue dark. *Papa!* he cried again.

I'm here, Akpa, his father called, swimming quickly to his side. Together they ventured out over the waves, following the pull of currents flowing south. Akpa's father slowed his pace and Akpa swam hard to keep up. The cliffs got smaller and smaller, then disappeared into a glittering wilderness of stars. They swam on and on for many days.

One day, a glistening narwhal came gliding though the sea beside them. His long ivory tusk seemed to measure the waves.

Do you know how far it is to our winter home? Akpa asked.

The whale slowed and drew a watery breath. *Oh, it's not so far from here to there,* he said in a soft, wet voice, *if you pay attention to the journey. Just keep your pointy end headed in the right direction,* he advised as he touched his tusk to Akpa's bill and slipped beneath the waves.

Another day, Akpa and his father came upon a strange, fat animal that was pulling himself up onto an iceberg with his teeth.

What kind of bird are you? Akpa asked, peering curiously at his wrinkled flippers.

The big leathery beast flopped onto the ice with a weighty sigh. *Tusk, tusk,* he grumbled, from beneath his bristly moustache. *I'm not a bird, I'm a walrus!* He squinted down at Akpa with his tiny pink eyes. *Like you, I may not fly,* the walrus said, *but I use the strength I have to lift myself toward the sky!*

Some days later, Akpa and his father came swimming through a drifting field of ice. In the day's last light, the sea was a labyrinth of blue and white. A harp seal surfaced, her coat like cloud-shadowed snow. *Where are you going?* Akpa asked the seal.

The same place as you, the seal replied.

But how do you find your way? Akpa wondered, for she was all alone, and the world was growing dark.

I follow the light, the seal replied, lifting her face toward the stars.

Do the stars know the way to our winter home? Akpa wondered.

The seal paused and searched the evening sky, then pointed toward a solitary star. *See that star?* she asked. *That is* Nuuttuittuq, *the star that doesn't move. Keep its light at your back and you will find your way.*

23

And so, Akpa and his father swam on, with the glimmering star behind them. At night, lantern fish filled the sea with their soft blue glow, as if lighting the way to a secret land beneath the waves. Seaweed forests bent and swayed, and pale belugas drifted silently by. The moon covered its face with clouds, then filled the sky with its silvery light.

As the days passed, Akpa's feathers grew long and glossy. At the same time, his father's worn feathers fell away to reveal bright winter ones. Beneath the waves, fish darted like silver needles sewing a silky blue gown. Akpa's father taught his son to dive down after them. And while his wings couldn't yet carry him above the waves, Akpa learned to soar beneath them. Holding his breath and chasing after fish, Akpa grew braver, and stronger, and faster.

Akpa learned many things on their long sea voyage, and now the north wind carried the smell of snow and ice. *Ukiuliruut,* the edge of winter, was close behind. Each day, Akpa watched with longing as young murres traced brief lines across the sky. They seemed to call to Akpa: *Come with us! Come with us!* The air rustled with their beating wings as, one by one, they lifted up to finish their journey south upon the wind.

You are ready too, Akpa, his father said one evening. *Come fly with me.* Then, smiling gently at his son, he began to beat his wings into the wind and rise up over the waves. *Remember,* he called, *sometimes you have to leap when you can't yet fly, and trust that the wind will carry you!*

As Akpa watched his father fly higher, the way from sea to sky seemed impossibly far. Then, thinking back on his adventure, Akpa's heart began to fill with everything he'd learned along the way. *Oh, it's not so far from here to there,* the narwhal had said, *if you pay attention to the journey. I'm not a bird!* the walrus had said. *But I am!* Akpa said out loud, holding out his stubby wings. Then, looking down at his legs, Akpa was surprised to see how strong they'd grown from swimming all that way. *I may not fly,* the walrus had said, *but I use the strength I have to lift myself toward the sky.*

Slowly at first, then faster and faster, Akpa began to beat his wings with all his strength. As he flapped his wings, he pushed his legs to run as hard as he could across the waves. And as he ran and flapped, the wind picked up, seeming to offer a helping hand. Then with one great push, Akpa skimmed across the waves, bouncing like a skipping stone. With a second big push his feet brushed the wave tops and he began lifting up! Up! *Up!* Akpa watched the ocean fall away as he rose higher and higher into the air. He could fly!

Papa! he cried, *Papa!* As his father slowed his pace, Akpa beat his wings hard to catch up.

One day, Akpa would fly back to the wild and icy land from which he'd come. But for now, Akpa and his father kept the light of the guiding star behind them. Together they climbed into the sky.

Endnote

Sometimes called "the penguins of the Arctic," thick-billed murres are black and white seabirds that spend their entire lives at sea, returning to land only to breed. At their remote Arctic and subarctic nesting sites, thick-billed murres gather in noisy colonies of many thousands. Here, on the bare, narrow ledges of towering sea cliffs, each murre pair lays but one freckled egg. High on the sea cliffs, murre eggs are safe from most predators. Both parents take turns keeping their egg warm and, once hatched, both care for, feed, and protect the chick.

When murre chicks are only three weeks old and unable to fly, they leap from sea cliffs that can be over 500 metres (1,640 feet) high and begin swimming south with their male parents. In this extraordinary swimming migration, murre chicks from colonies in the eastern Canadian Arctic and western Greenland swim the first 1,000 kilometres (621 miles) of their journey south to their wintering grounds off the coasts of Newfoundland and Labrador. No other bird species on earth travels so far while still unable to fly. Along the way, chicks learn to fend for themselves in the open ocean, and when they are about a month and a half old, they learn to fly.

Thick-billed murres live for up to thirty years. They mate for life, and breed on the same small span of cliff ledge year after year. While many of their colonies lie within Arctic protected areas, thick-billed murres remain vulnerable to changes in the Arctic marine environment brought about by climate change, increasing industrial activity, and marine pollution.

Range Map

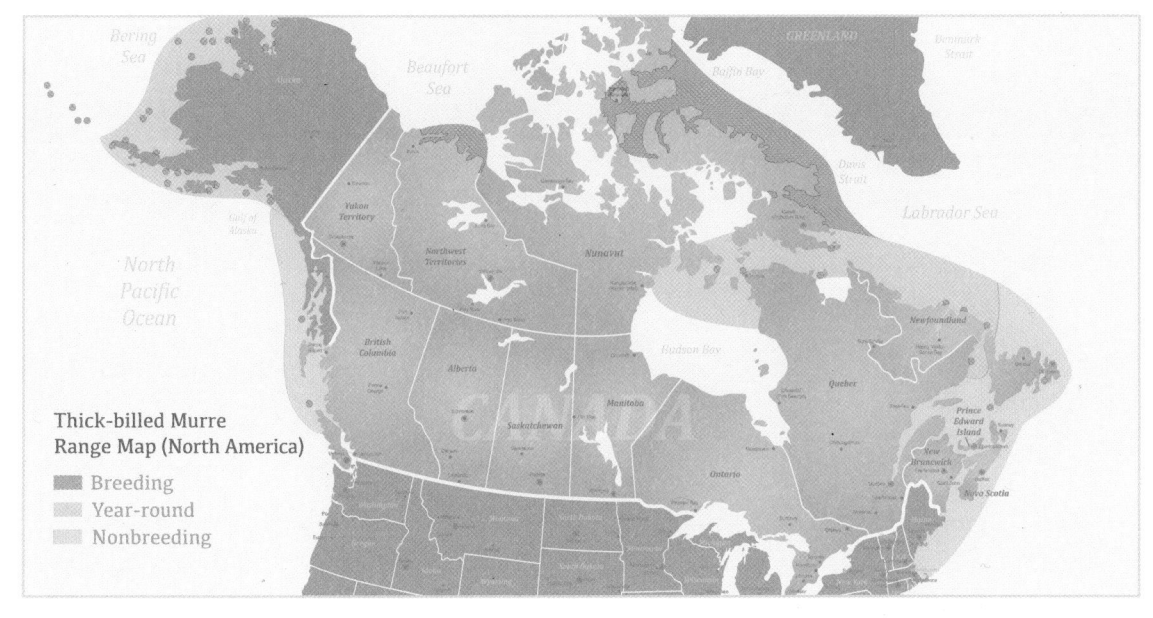

Thick-billed Murre
Range Map (North America)
- Breeding
- Year-round
- Nonbreeding

Glossary of Inuktut Words

Inuktut is the term for Inuit languages spoken in Canada, including Inuktitut and Inuinnaqtun. The pronunciation guides in this book are intended to support non-Inuktut speakers in their reading of Inuktut words. These pronunciations are not exact representations of how the words are pronounced by Inuktut speakers. For more resources on how to pronounce Inuktut words, visit inhabitmedia.com/inuitnipingit.

Term	Pronunciation	Meaning
akpa	AHK-pah	thick-billed murre
manniit	MAHN-neet	springtime
Nuuttuittuq	NOO-too-ee-took	the north star
ukiuliruut	ook-ee-oo-lee-ROOT	the edge of winter heading south

Mia Pelletier studied ecology and anthropology and holds an MSc from the Durrell Institute of Conservation and Ecology in the United Kingdom. Drawn to wilderness and shorelines, Mia has lived in faraway places from California to the Magdalen Islands and the Canadian Arctic, and spent six years working on the co-management of Arctic protected areas with Inuit communities on Baffin Island. She is the author of *Avati: Discovering Arctic Ecology*, *A Children's Guide to Arctic Birds*, and *A Children's Guide to Arctic Butterflies*, which received a 2020 John Burrough's Riverby Award for exceptional natural history books for children.

Kagan McLeod has been illustrating for magazines, newspapers, and design firms since 1999, after graduating from Sheridan College's illustration program. He began work as a staff artist for the *National Post* newspaper, and has had illustration work published in *Entertainment Weekly*, *Reader's Digest*, *The Walrus*, *The Wall Street Journal*, *Toronto Life*, *The Boston Globe*, and *Popular Mechanics*. His first graphic novel, *Infinite Kung Fu*, was published in 2012. He lives in Toronto with his wife, two daughters, and a hound dog.

INHABIT MEDIA
IQALUIT • TORONTO